Hervé Guibert

My
Manservant
and Me

T0017170

madcap novel

Hervé Guibert

My Manservant and Me

Translated by

Jeffrey Zuckerman

Nightboat Books
New York

Copyright © 1991 by Éditions du Seuil
Translation Copyright © 2022
by Jeffrey Zuckerman
Foreword Copyright © 2022
by Shiv Kotecha

ISBN: 978-1-64362-152-4

Cover art: detail from Hervé Guibert,
Autoportrait à la chaise, n.d.
© Christine Seemuller-Guibert.
Courtesy of the Estate of Hervé Guibert, Paris,
and Les Douches la Galerie, Paris

Design and typesetting by
Rissa Hochberger
Typeset in Caslon 540

Cataloging-in-publication data is
available from the Library of Congress

Nightboat Books
New York
www.nightboat.org

Contents

Fresh Hell

A *foreword by*
Shiv
Kotecha

"How to last? P.C. asked a journalist one day during an interview, not out of opportunism. How to last, that is the question, since one damages oneself into one's own work."

—HERVÉ GUIBERT,
The Mausoleum of Lovers (1987-88)[1]

The 1990 publication of *To the Friend Who Did Not Save My Life*—Hervé Guibert's candid *roman à clef* about a fake AIDS vaccine—made the novelist, photographer, and AIDS victim both rich and famous. He gave interviews on national TV, and his toothsome blue-eyed face appeared in magazines and on *affiches* plastered across Paris. During the subsequent two years, Guibert made his proximity to death the subject of four more novels and a hospital diary.

He also produced *La Pudeur ou l'impudeur* (*Modesty or Immodesty*), an hour-long home video in which he documents himself craning his arms into pajamas, shooting diarrhea, and play-acting a suicide attempt, as if bent on disarming and satisfying the tumescent sympathies of a liberal French middle class who had become perversely invested in watching him, their resident AIDS patient, perish in real time. In December 1991, a month before his video diary aired on the television network TF1, a botched suicide attempt and complications with the virus led to Guibert's actual death at the age of thirty-six.

My Manservant and Me, translated into English for the first time by Jeffrey Zuckerman, is the last novel Guibert saw published in his lifetime. In it, Guibert continues to upend the expectations of his readers, and turns his sneering rictus to a future of aging and decrepitude he knew he would not live to see. Dated "Kyoto-Anchorage-Paris. January–February 2036," the narrative outlines the violent, though occasionally kinky, relationship between a former theater director, aged eighty—who lives in a luxury residence on Paris's rue de Varenne as heir to a "colossal fortune" but has zero friends—and the teenage boy he's hired to care for his frail, farting body. In 1993, Edmund White praised *My Manservant and Me*, calling it Guibert's "most successful invention"— in that without explicitly mentioning AIDS, Guibert told the truth about the body's decline and the humiliation that accompanies the contractual interdependence between a patient and their caretaker.[2] To be exact, Guibert doesn't offer a positive account of disability but instead uses an onslaught of slurs to make an unrelenting and derisory hellscape of terminal illness. White highlights Guibert's desire to provoke, drawing a contrast between Guibert and his American and who is not from Paris and ambiguously raced; he's described as having "yellow eyes" and a "very peculiar way of speaking." We learn that his escape from Mettray—the remote penal colony Jean Genet spent three years in as a teen—was occasioned by a derelict, neorealist filmmaker who cast the pimpled orphan as his non-professional lead in an artsy straight-to-VHS flop. Eventually, we learn too about the private mutiny he enacts on his employer's body, and about his masterful grift of the old man's morphine and financial estate. "Brutality is on the rise everywhere," he explains, before urinating on his patient. Guibert waits till the end to disclose that his name is Jim (which I cannot dissociate from the enslaved Black man of Twain's *The Adventures of Huckleberry Finn*) and his unsparing method of attack: "I won't stop talking to Sir"—Jim tells his comatose master, whose pen he's nabbed to finish their cowritten story—"so that your brain of a shriveled white imaginary: "Budapesti tavern servers in white clothes and golden buttons, Moroccan bellhops with fezzes, Japanese taxi drivers wearing cotton gloves, La Coupole waiters tucking tea towels into those pants' low-slung, tight-cinched waist." On the level of parody, the colonized subjects appear as world-building devices—reduced to décor. But as elements of realism, they read as ill-wrought projections of the fantasies—both sexual and domestic—that Guibert's two characters imagine one another enjoying. In one episode, the master gifts Jim with a sex holiday in Thailand so that he may have "a memory of a massage just like everybody else." Jim is unmoved by the gesture, but the sheer fact of travel revivifies the old man, who cannot see beyond their own composite likenesses: "When we, my manservant and me, go out together on Bangkok's streets, after the rains have stopped, I'm under the illusion of constantly seeing us in a huge mirror that a slave would be carrying on his back while bounding ahead of us." In another episode, Jim nurses his master's striated racial hang-ups by admitting to his own: "I'd hire a Japanese manservant, because they're more subservient than we are." Slavishness being reflexive, at the novel's end, even the most repugnant aspects of the master—his racism, ableism, and misogyny—become part of the couple's shared, stained surface.

Guibert's *My Manservant and Me*, in this sense, serves as a counterpoint to the longstanding tradition of European men using gay, liberatory literature as a pretext to extol the receptive sexual hospitalities of non-European peoples. There's the case of Roland Barthes's *Incidents*, for example, in which the writer gives an epithet to each of the Mohammads he tries to sleep with on a trip to Morocco, lest he is unable to remember them: "Un Mohammed," "Mohammed Gymnastique,""Mohammed (évidement)," and so forth.[4] And there is Renaud Camus, who, before becoming the primary architect of the malevolent conspiracy theory known as "The Great Replacement," which claims that white, Christian Europe is under siege by Black and Brown immigrants from North and sub-Saharan Africa, was known for his erotic memoir *Tricks* (1979), detailing the sex he has with twenty-five strangers across various global metropoles. In his introduction to the volume, Barthes lauded Camus's closeted politic as well as his sterile prose style, commending the writer for eliding mention of "homosexuality" and for "neutralizing" his depictions of sex between men: "[Camus's fictions] do not participate in the game of interpretation. They are surfaces without shadows, without ulterior motives."[5] Unlike these men, Guibert refuses comforting representations of homosexual desire and of relational bankruptcy alike,

NOTES

[1] Hervé Guibert, *Mausoleum of Lovers: Journals 1976-1991*, trans. Nathanaël (New York: Nightboat, 2014), 562.

[2] Edmund White, "Love Stories," *London Review of Books*, November 4, 1993. https://www.lrb.co.uk/the-paper/v15/n21/edmund-white/love-stories.

[3] White, Ibid.

[4] Roland Barthes, *Incidents* (Paris: Éditions du Seuil, 1987), 27, 38, 43. On the posthumous reception history of Barthes's publication, see D.A. Miller's *Bringing Out Roland Barthes* (Oakland: University of California Press, 1992). See also: Mehammed Amadeus Mack's extraordinary scholarship on interethnic relationships in Franco-Arab literature in his book *Sexagon: Muslims, France, and the Sexualization of National Culture* (New York: Fordham University Press, 2017).

[5] Ralph Sarkonak, *Angelic Echoes: Hervé Guibert and Company* (University of Toronto Press, 2000), 233.

[6] Camus initially developed the idea of the Great Replacement in his 2010 publication *L'Abécédaire de l'in-nocence* (Abecedarium of no-harm), followed by the eponymous publication *Le Grand Remplacement: introduction au remplacisme global* in 2011. The volume is not translated in English but its resonances are deeply felt, as in the rallying cries of the white supremacists that gathered for the Unite the Right rally in Charlottesville, Virginia of August 2017; "They will not replace us," is one of Camus's principal mottoes.

My Manservant and Me

*To Christine, who cut out a maga-
zine photo of my character for me
on the Anchorage–Tokyo flight, and
to whom I fear this story will mean
nothing at all.*

I never imagined that my manservant might like me. In fact, I thought, upon making him my manservant, that he would hate me. He was a lazy young man who, by chance, had snagged the leading role in a film and whom no director had contacted since. How unwise it proved for me to decide, that afternoon, to go see a movie at the theater.

First I'd thought about hiring, since neither my secretary nor my steward could take on such a role, and since I was farting more and more violently at those high-society soirées that I barely ever went to anymore, some elegant young man who would follow my footsteps in public, but act as if he didn't know me, like a magician's assistant, doing his best to blush, to cough, to discreetly apologize instead of me every time I let out one of those machine-gun gusts.

I'd imagined that whenever I brought this young man to a restaurant to keep me company after his workday, that by silent agreement we'd have decided that he would, without fail, insist to the maître d' that he wasn't the least bit hungry, and that with the tip of my lips, as if I didn't want to burn myself, I would nibble at the glaze on an especially heavy dish, which I would then slide across the table toward my underling, who would wolf it down greedily. Unfortunately, nothing went as expected.

And then I'd been keen on some Pakistani steward who wouldn't speak French, and therefore wouldn't understand a thing when I was on the phone. I'd been set on keeping what remained of my personal life discreet; the help is so quick to gossip with neighbors and storekeepers. But I don't have many people to talk to anymore, much less anyone to keep from understanding me. All my real friends have died, the last one less than two weeks ago.

The narrators of Russian novels have manservants who sleep like dogs in drafty antechambers, sharpen their foils for dueling, and wear their old overcoats. They're failures, often counterparts to their masters, and could have stood in their stead had some accident of birth or some setback, some lady, sheer fate, not relegated them to this rank. They've been worn down into servility, all their being exudes something rancid. They work without any love, any attentiveness, not even waxing their masters' boots can spark their enthusiasm.

My own manservant was a killer lying in wait; that was why I'd chosen him.

I was a man in decline. I needed a true bodyguard, someone who would pull me upright when I fell, get me dressed, massage my legs when they were so swollen that I couldn't feel them anymore.

My manservant was the polar opposite of the usual Russian manservant: he carried out the least obligation with zeal, as if this act, in this case getting me out of my bathtub, was of the most vital interest to him. Maybe it was the fervor of hatred that drove him; there was no way for me to know at that point.

Did he at least have his eyes on my inheritance? I myself had been the beneficiary of my great-grandfather's colossal fortune, and I already had an astronomical number of nephews and nieces, great-nephews and great-nieces, the men embassy secretaries and marketing directors and lawyers, the women press agents and art dealers. I felt no affinity for this brood, and I knew that, unless I pulled some unlikely trick, for example adopting my manservant, it would be those more or less detested nephews and nieces who would inherit some of my great-grandfather's fortune which I'd already started frittering away on these trips to the other end of the world with my manservant.

That said—and I don't even consider myself all that miserly—I do like to travel economy. Even from Paris to Rome, I take the 895-franc Nouvelles Frontières charter flight. People in second class turn out to be far more easygoing than in first. I've always been good at deceiving anybody around me. The two of us, my manservant and me, went virtually unnoticed. We seemed like two guys as young as everyone else, like two brothers. I'm eighty years old but on the plane I'll wear cushioned Nike tennis shoes, tight jeans, leather jackets, my Ray-Bans hiding my crow's feet and my hat the scalpel's touch-ups from the facelifts I've undergone every five years without fail since I turned forty; exfoliating costs more than the actual operation, as in any case it'll all have to go under the knife again. I feel like I'm young for a second time. On my Walkman, I'm listening to the same music as my manservant, some rap I can barely get my head around, I'm chewing the same gum and its flavors are the same sickening ones.

My manservant is a gem. He would never, not with any apologetic glance offered to some young woman stunned by the unlikely couple we made, or some other kid trying to figure out his involvement, betray my true age, which he certainly isn't unaware of as he takes off my shoes, unobtrusively lifts me out of too-deep seats I had to sit in, almost pulls on himself the sleeves of my jacket become too heavy to shoulder, and administers my injections into these bony limbs where there's nothing left to prick.

I've been distraught since I was twenty by the situation, the fundamental structure of servitude: does this mean I like to enslave others? Budapesti tavern servers in white clothes and golden buttons, Moroccan bellhops with fezzes, Japanese taxi drivers wearing cotton gloves, La Coupole waiters tucking tea towels into those pants' low-slung, tight-cinched waists have always struck me as the epitome of elegance—when their lot in life hasn't driven them to despair.

Why doesn't my manservant leave me? Sometimes I do wonder. He starred in the film when he was fifteen, but his director, set on keeping some mystery, convinced that this sudden miracle of an actor might strike audiences as unremarkable, barred him from doing press junkets, going on Drucker's or Sabatier's shows as he'd always hoped to, posing for fashion shoots, or answering pretty journalists' self-aggrandizing questions. The director, determined not to be outshone, as he was a man who commanded plenty of attention himself, thrust forward this fifteen-year-old total unknown as a hero and yanked him right back into the shadows so that he would be immediately forgotten behind some hazy memory of his character. I have to confess I feel no sympathy for the director in question, he's the one who, in a way, found my manservant, not I, even though I'd have been proud if I had. I didn't make my manservant prove himself before I hired him: a simple gentleman's agreement bound us to one another.

Now my manservant is twenty; at this point nobody would recognize him on the street or recall his character in that mediocre film which never aired on TV but which we still have on a videotape that we sometimes take some pleasure in watching. My manservant hadn't aspired to or even imagined a career as an actor. He would more likely, had I not popped up, have become a mechanic or a truck driver. A simple soul, but a devious one as he's stayed at my beck and call for four years.

He's the one who had the wonder-ful idea to pass me off as a boy like himself. He said one day: "If you'll allow me, Sir, it's true that for your age, if you really are as old as you say, you've got a super-young face, but your threads, Sir, they're all wrong. Houndstooth jackets, square-end knitted ties, those bell-bottom pants, your camel-hair coats, you can't get tackier than that. You're whining and whining about how you can't walk anymore, why don't you wear Nikes like me instead of those horrible Berluti loafers that you say cost an arm and a leg and that I have to shine, if you'll allow me, Sir, every morning, when I could be of far greater use in other ways. You'll see that with Nike Airs you'll get your pep back, they're super comfy, you won't have all those cramps anymore, you won't need to hang onto my arm at the end of a walk. Shoes are like cars, they need a bit of suspension. Your wheezing old body doesn't have any anymore. I'm your suspension. With Nike Airs, you'll have built-in suspension."

I tried to insist on a uniform for my manservant; in the end, he insisted on one for me. I'd wavered between several sorts of outfits for him: it would really have been nice to see him in red or black livery with a round collar, huge gold- or silver-plated buttons, like those elevator attendants at Le

Train Bleu, playing up the way a lower back curves into a polyester-corseted derrière. It's no secret that homosexuals are drawn to uniforms—those of seamen, firefighters, legionnaires. As I've never been one, I've always been fascinated, almost erotically so, by the outfits that minions of all sorts wear. Down to the uniform, the saddest one in the world, of these harried beings one only ever sees on service stairways, brush and dustpan in hand, when the hotel elevator is broken, this pathetic striped apron tied off around a heavy, snow-white shirt collar. This apron spurs me to pat the head of these men usually too old to still be working, but there's no use considering that life can no longer bring them the least bit of comfort.

My manservant immediately rejected the uniform. He was almost seventeen at that point. He said: "Sir, forgive me, but I'm not wearing that uniform. I guess you've already won; if you tell me 'put on this suit or you're fired,' I'll put it on straightaway. But that's not going to happen, first because taking care of a uniform like this, which has to be spotless at all times, and has to be changed repeatedly, would be an unnecessary hassle and keep me from properly serving you. And if I start wearing a uniform, why would it be this one and not any other? Why wouldn't there be a proper uniform for each situation? Would I have to put on a pair of Public Hospitals of Paris scrubs to give you a massage, and a nurse's scrubs to administer your injections, a driver's suit coat and hat when we go for a ride, and while we're at it why not worn-out maid's slippers and a shopping bag when I buy groceries? Is the point to humiliate me?

Amsterdam. My most faithful actor was Dagmar Hildekniffe, the Finnish Jacqueline Maillan; she died onstage while performing one of my plays. Back then, I was convinced I had at least a teensy bit of a knack for situations, they were tied off with a bow on top like the critics used to say, perfect little bits of clockwork, but looking back I have to concede that these situations were absolutely contrived and ludicrous. I actually feel ashamed when I happen to see one of them on TV. I had the foresight to use a British pseudonym for them. I still haven't confessed to my manservant that I'm the one who wrote all the nonsense that has him bent over laughing whenever it crops up on *Au théâtre ce soir* with second-rate actors. Fortunately, I've never felt compelled to create a true work of art. Maybe someday I'll make something that will hold up if I'm able to simply describe the relationship binding me to my manservant, as I've begun doing, which worries me because I have to hide it from him, and I can only write when he's running errands or getting some money at the bank.

I've never had any problems with granting him authorization to handle my finances. He's permitted to withdraw fifteen thousand francs every two weeks for living expenses. My manservant got me into an argument with my Scottish accountant, who handles my interests in Edinburgh. He insisted this man was robbing me blind. The manservant wrote a very terse note, which he forced me to sign, ordering the delivery of all my Scotland-based assets, in cash, to my Worms account within one week. I have two bank accounts in Paris, one with Worms and the other with Lazard; my great-grandfather was the one to suggest it when I was little, in case one of the two banks went under. Kingsley, who was a sort of friend, and who stayed with me on the rue de Varenne each time he came to Paris, never responded; he did as he was told by the deadline my manservant had set.

Now it's my manservant who handles all my affairs. My sole concern is keeping secret the provenance of the money that the Society of Dramatic Authors and Composers sends me every six months as royalties for my plays; it was such a thorny matter that I even considered forbidding that they be performed at all. Every time my manservant hands me the financial statements and asks: "What's all this moolah? And tell me again what this SACD is anyway?" My answers are evasive: "It's my retirement." His response: "For someone who hasn't done a thing in his life, as you're so fond of saying, it's an awfully pretty penny you've made for your retirement, isn't it?"

It's also my manservant, from this point on, who advises on my stock sales. He says: "Sir might do well to sell off his Fnac shares and buy some in Virgin. I would also recommend that Sir invest five hundred thousand francs in McDonald's as swiftly as he can." "How much is that in old francs?" I ask. "Fifty briques." "What's McDonald's, anyway? Some sort of Scottish thing? If I'm going to deal with the United Kingdom, why not go with blue chips, Burberry's or Old England?" "Sir, nobody bothers with Burberry's these days, you're completely out of touch, trust me on this, I haven't wiped out your fortune so far, have I?" My manservant had me swap my Institut Mérieux shares for Toshiba and my Laboratoire

Bellon shares for Mitsubishi, he says these are the companies of the future. He's converted all my dollars to yen. My manservant hates the Japanese, calls them ant-people, then insists that's exactly why they're such a sure bet. He says: "If I were a business-man, I'd only deal with the Japanese, I'd handle imports and exports at all levels. If I were a master myself, I'd hire a Japanese manservant, because they're more subservient than we are, and I'd enjoy making him suffer trials and tribulations the likes of which Sir has never imagined. The Japanese are masochists, it's in their blood, Sir, just like their slanty eyes. Masochism is an energy one should know how to channel." Yes, my manservant says unbelievable things like that.

My manservant gets along rather well with my Worms banker, Renaud de La Martinière, a raving lunatic. That specifically was why I'd chosen him as my banker, long before getting the idea, when I saw that film he'd acted in, to hire my manservant. In the middle of our first meeting, at my place, in the green lounge, Renaud de La Martinière said: "Leave all your money with me, I'll turn it all into air. It's always going to be worth less and less, I can give you my word on this, because money is worthless. The only thing that has any value these days are compromising photos taken in one's youth, stashed away in safe-deposit boxes. Photos where you're posing like one of those French girls, if you catch my drift." "No, I don't," I said, "there aren't any photos like that from my past, considering that I've never, and you can mark my words, never, not even when I was a very little boy, ever let anyone take a picture of me, certainly not by my father who was an esteemed photographer, and much less dressed up like a girl." "But an invaluable asset, for a man," insisted Renaud de La Martinière, whose strangeness had me ready to hire him on the spot, "is having nice, perfectly toned legs, silky-smooth, waxed if needed, legs you'd be proud to show off on the beach or at the pool." On the walls of Renaud de La Martinière's Worms office, where we had our meetings before my manservant took my place, were photos of a very beautiful woman who no doubt would have delighted me when I was younger had I not been aware that she was actually a man, with splendid legs, taut and stilettoed, sheathed in fishnet stockings, her ankles bound with leather straps, a dominatrix of sorts. I'm one of only a few in on the secret, aware that this lady is none other than Renaud de La Martinière himself. His financial partners, own, when I don't call him, to watch me sleep, to make sure all is well, to check my breathing, and, when he can't quite make it out, to ever so gently raise my arm to take my pulse, or just to press his ear to my heart to listen to its beating. He never talks about it, but I've come to understand that he's terribly afraid I might die in the middle of the night, in my sleep, even though that's the best thing that could possibly happen to me. And that my family would then, in order to collect my fortune, accuse him of having suffocated me with a pillow or having given me too large a dose of my injection. An eighty-year-old man has to die at some point. It's odd, in the wee hours, to open my eyes a little and see my manservant standing beside me, in a dressing gown or the bathrobe I wore when I was young, if not naked beneath the fur coat I'd had made for Moscow, observing me, in the half-darkness, without saying a word, his yellow eyes fixed on me. Sometimes he scares me.

I'm no longer allowed to go into my manservant's bedroom, my former bedroom, where he sleeps in my great-grandmother's canopy bed. My great-grandmother and my great-grandfather, too, had separate bedrooms. I don't know what my manservant's getting up to in my former bedroom, he says he has nothing of his own, and yet he needs, if nothing else, a place all to himself where nobody can go in. He calls it his den, or his foxhole. A sixty-square-meter Regency-era den. I'd be interested in slipping in there one day to see how he's done it up.

My manservant dismissed all my staff, my former secretary and my house-keeper, he says it was just throwing money out the window, that they were incompetent, lazy people. My housekeeper and my secretary are claiming he chased them out with a sharpened knife, but I wasn't there to see it. My manservant wants to take care of everything himself, he points out that he's not illiterate and he's perfectly capable of running a household, even one this big, all on his own. I have to concede that he's saving me a driver, a masseur, a nurse, a bellhop when I travel, and certainly a maid and a secretary, all while remaining the most devoted personal manservant ever to live, even when he's throwing horrific tantrums.

The other day, with a single blow, he destroyed my Sony Trinitron that I'd had him shell out 6990 francs for two weeks earlier at Darty, his excuse being that we'd had a ridiculous little disagreement. I wanted to watch a variety show, and he wanted to watch soccer. He said that variety shows are just a distraction for our times, that they dull our wits, debase us, he had a whole theory about it, but on the other hand soccer is invigorating to watch, absolutely pure. And then he'd rammed his fist into the device, blood, bandages, he couldn't do a thing for a week, no cooking or cleaning. Nothing to eat, no more TV, my cigars confiscated, my flask of vodka squirreled away, I was bedridden, horribly depressed. Even just lying on the couch was something my manservant wouldn't allow me. "What do we have here," he said. "Is Sir really abed at this hour? That's unhealthy. Sir will just sink into the bed. Take my hand, on, at eleven years old, he was off-loaded to the Mettray colony, a reformatory. He showed me a scratched-up little photo of himself back then: buzz cut, scowling face, pimply cheeks, the kind of anthropometric photo doctors used to take against yardsticks. My manservant told me that at Mettray children slept in uncomfortable hammocks hung from spartan wood planks topped by crucifixes and Virgin Marys, arranged military-style so they could all spy on each other and rat each other out, watched and beaten by old ex-cons as they taught and abused children, my manservant added in a wistful tone. Mettray was where this director, who clearly wouldn't go down in the history of film, had auditioned boys and plucked out my rare bird. I should have had that idea first: to go and pick out my manservant at Mettray, and hire him directly without any cinematic intermediary, which had only defiled him, he said, and taught

My manservant has never cut me while shaving me. He could have, and I wouldn't have said a thing, but he's careful. I can't get my arm all the way up to my chin anymore. My manservant shaves me by the book, he starts by draping a pistachio-green nylon barber's cape over me, taping a sterile gauze collar around my neck below my Adam's apple, unfolds the long razor blade from its ebony handle, and starts to strop it, with a mechanical flick of the wrist, against the rubber strap, powders me, scrapes me, and cauterizes all irritations with the right lotions, oil for my neck, alcohol for my cheeks. My manservant is an expert at shaving, an inspired yet punctilious inventor, he says he picked it up while in the army, even though he knows perfectly well that he didn't serve, because of me in fact, without knowing it because he dreamed of enlisting in the Marines or the Air Force, but he was too young, and he keeps forget I only have one left, a sore spot for me. He acts like I've always had all of them, and no dentures, even though he's the one who brushes them every night, and brings them back to me every morning in the glass of water that I pretend to drink, even as he immediately looks away. Once, however, my manservant declared something that caught me off guard: "Sir, I'm not joking when I say this: I'm ready to give you my teeth, to trade your device for my teeth which a dentist will have to pull out one by one by and graft onto your gums, that way you'll have a smile that's not so rigid as the one with your dentures, and I can just fill my mouth with gold." I didn't take him up on the offer, I just responded: "What a funny little idea! But don't you care about having your own teeth? A young man's stiff smile is far more unbearable than an old man's." My manservant cut me off: "How could Sir have possibly thought I was serious?" And he drew my bath. I don't smile at my manservant anymore. He's just as discreet when it comes to bathing me as to brushing my teeth. He never looks at my emaciated body, it's as if I don't have one, his eyes might pass over it but they never land on anything, they slide right past, like an ectoplasm. I'm always cold, so he rubs my feet vigorously with the towel, saying: "I'm giving Sir child's feet again." Similarly prudent with my dangling genitals and my wrinkly butt, he wipes them down with a towel, efficiently, repeating each time: "There we are." I feel like he's rubbing a chiffon cloth over some Chinese furniture, I'm a black console table that's always a bit dusty.

"Why don't you pen your memoirs?" my manservant asks. "It'd keep you busy, I'd finally learn a bit about you, and you'd stop bellyaching all day long." My answer is that my life isn't interesting at all, that I've never done anything worth writing home about, never rubbed shoulders with famous faces, that even my trips have been cookie-cutter, nothing more interesting than the commercialized pleasures of Club Med. He still has no idea that I've started to set down our story. He says: "What about your romances? Why don't you talk about your romances? Now that'd be a real page-turner." I wonder if he's pulling my leg, I tell him that I was no great shakes there either, that my conquests were actually rather pitiful and that my recollections are so hazy that I can't even be sure they're mine.

My manservant always wants to stick the thermometer under my arm, whereas I prefer it in the butt like in the good old days. I don't have enough muscle to hold it tight in my armpit, it slips, I never get any higher than thirty-five degrees Celsius. Even taking his temperature, even with a bit of a fever. My anus stays warm when my body is numb with cold. My manservant says those are barbaric, outdated habits, not hygienic at all, that only the French would do filthy things like that, shoving suppositories up there, that Germans and Spaniards aren't half as twisted, their cultures notwithstanding. And yet my manservant is utterly set on mustard-seed poultices, and he uses the least bit of chest pain to hammer the point home. It's icy and wet on my skin, then it warms up little by little, it burns, it becomes intolerable, I beg him to take it off. "Keep it on a bit longer," my manservant says,

All I subsist on now is Munich beer and aquavit. My doctor tells my man-servant every time he leads him to the door, they whisper but I'm not as hard of hearing as they think, that malnutrition this severe means I've only got a few more weeks, or some-times he puts it otherwise and says: "You should consider the prospect of these being your final months." But alcohol does my body good. My manservant says it's infused my flesh, and my skin smells like ether. I bloat up. First it was my feet, then my legs, then the fingers of my hand, my fingernails popped off under this pressure of swollen flesh. I have crab-claws of a sort rather than hands, and wooden clogs instead of feet. I can't pull on my slippers or my gloves any-more when we head out in the Skoda. I picked this Czech car because it was the cheapest, and, more than that, the most versatile. With my SACD royal-ties I could buy a Rolls-Royce, but it's

I decided to give my manservant a trip to Bangkok for Christmas, a fond childhood memory of mine, a memory of a massage just like everyone else. We went to the penthouse at Hilltop. I booked a suite with two separate apartments so as not to be in each other's way should my manservant feel tempted, as I myself had hoped in vain for the last ten years, to have a romp or two; it'd be easy here. All these young women are like flowers, ready to open up. It's monsoon season. When it's really pouring, the deluge comes through the French doors and floods the carpeting, we roll out paper towels for the joins. The deluge comes all at once, several times a day, drenches everything, and stops almost as quickly, the village down below turns blue and gray again, all a-twinkle, mottled, and smoky in its post-rain steam. I wanted to take my manservant to Shangri-La, which at my time was the absolute height of luxury, but it didn't stir up any excitement on his part, I watched him out the corner of my eye, he ogled all these girls vacantly, without any disgust, without any desire either, just as he might glance at the bottom of his glass of gin before finishing it off, somewhat melancholically, as if nothing was to come after these girls' bodies under the spotlights spinning around metal bars, nothing left to look forward to, nothing left to await, nothing left to drink. I whispered to him: "They go for a song, I'll buy you one, just pick, you can head up to your rooms with her, you can spend as long as you like, I'll wait." He demurred, he said: "I'm not going to leave Sir all alone in a place like that, I'd rather we go bowling." In

Bangkok's bowling alleys it's children who pick up the pins, ugly children, no good for prostitution, all that can be seen of them is their bare, skinny legs darting behind the panels from one lane to the next.

I think all the madness of the cloud-bursts has been getting on my man-servant's nerves, like explosions. On a whim, he went down to be shaved, like at Mettray, he said, at the hotel barber. When he came back up, I saw that he had a scar on his scalp, like the arc of a trepanning scar, which I'd never noticed given his shock of hair. Maybe someone had cut one of his cranial nerves, the one for desire. I brought him here so he could pick up a thing or two, but he showed no inter-est for the girls or the guys, his eyes would land on them in the street as if they were sacred cows or baby strollers. I'd have gotten pretty fed up if I'd been planning to use him to accost a few girls. Was I dealing with a simpleton, or was he just putting on an act for reasons I couldn't fathom? He'd had me trade my double-cushioned green Nikes that I felt like I'd been flying on for purportedly more stylish Palladiums that were better against snakes and scorpions. It's stupid, though, there are no scorpions here, or snakes.

When we, my manservant and me, go out together on Bangkok's streets, after the rains have stopped, I'm under the illusion of constantly seeing us in a huge mirror that a slave would be carrying on his back while bounding ahead of us. I can tell the two of us apart with our similar outfits, but sometimes I'm no longer so sure if it's him on the left and me on the right, as if we were a single person now doubled. Sometimes I also catch us in the mirror transformed into women. It's a rather madcap picture. My manservant is a lady-in-waiting dressed in black, a sort of dismal Little Drear Riding Hood, and I'm a hulking beanpole teetering in my bleached pleather thigh-high boots, my scrawny butt wedged into black tights with nothing but a leather jacket covering them, and long flowing artificial red locks gathered in a kerchief that, with its tight knot, also covers my cheeks, I'm wearing opaque wraparound sunglasses, I know I'm eighty years old, but from a distance I could pass for eighteen, and this delusion never stops making me smile.

"How'd you manage to filch your great-grandfather's inheritance?" my manservant asked me once we were back from Thailand. I was stunned, to buy myself some time I asked him to repeat the question. "Whatever put that idea in your head?" I stammered. "It's quite simple, Sir, as you know: when one agrees to serve a master of your kind, one seeks out vice. No matter what it takes, we don't sleep until we've ferreted it out. And when we finally lay our eyes on it, it's astonishing how much we're at ease. We've got you hook, line, and sinker, and even though we're still respectful of you, we know who's got the upper hand. In short, the master should never know that his manservant has uncovered his vice, otherwise he'll catch a fright and abdicate his role." "What's this jibber-jabber, where are you getting all this malarkey about misappropriation of inheritances?" "I have to wonder why you've held onto your great-grandfather's will, is it because you've got a bad conscience about it, is it Exhibit A of your remorse? It's plain as day, though, the paper in question is deeply compromising, you should have torn it up." For a few seconds I was convinced he wanted to blackmail me. But no, on the contrary: "Well, if you're not going to tear it up yourself, I'll do the tearing up for you." "But how did you dig it up?" "What do you think I've been doing while you take your endless mid-afternoon naps? Dusting the shelves? Of course not, sir, I've been rummaging. Rummaging through everything. I was looking for vice. I upended everything and then put it all back just so. Now, thanks to all your papers, I can reconstruct the entirety of your life, from cradle to grave, the looming grave. Your old great-grandfather can't have been too fond of you if he left everything to the Humane Society. A dirty trick, that. But your machinations were far worse: you despoiled a charitable gift, and betrayed your great-grandfather's final wishes. He'd be red with rage, no question of it, if he had any idea that the money he'd been setting aside all his life had gone straight to you, a wicked great-grandson, a young cynical dandy." Cynical dandy: I recognized that phrase from the very beginning of my notebook, proof that he'd read it, but I didn't say anything. He went on: "Do I have it right that, as long as I've been with you, it's presumably been thanks to the assistance of some fly-by-night lawyer that a huge scam has covered my room and board and paid for these pointless, cockamamie trips that haven't done me the least good? It's just a kennel of our own. Imagine that, leaving everything to the animals! Rail-thin stray dogs, howling in hunger until they're shot dead. Creatures need love, too, Sir."

thing. To entice him they'd offered him a tidy little sum that would have allowed him to rent a room during the film shoot, and abandon me. I glanced over the screenplay before throwing it in the trash, in my heart and head, with the accompanying letter: it was just the sequel to the previous film, my manservant was a few years older, he was no longer the miscreant, he was doing his best to fit into society. But whereas the first director simply made mediocre psychological dramas, this one was clearly a voyeuristic faggot. Each situation was a pretext to bare a shoulder, or some other body part, ahead of the inevitable shower scene. That would have upset my boy. No evidence of this proposal, which I was afraid would be raised anew, could remain here, apart from this paper on which I write, but I have to confess that from now on I'd be loath to tear it up, I'm starting to develop a

taste for this habit I hadn't even con-
templated for the past eighty years.

It was a dramatic turn of events I
couldn't have possibly dreamed up
when I still had a head for such things.
My manservant came into the sitting
room and said: "Sir, I've found us a
very nice Picasso at the FIAC, I need
seventy million francs." I had no idea
my manservant had been prowling the
International Contemporary Art Fair
when he was supposed to be at the market. I said: "Seventy million francs?
Old ones or new ones?" Sometimes I
suspected my manservant was taking
advantage of my confusion between
new francs and old francs. "New, of
course," he declared. "But then, how
many old francs is that?" I was trying to buy myself some time to find

a somewhat credible parry. My manservant thought for a few seconds, then hit me with the fateful number: "That comes to seven billion in your system. But I've already saved up five hundred thousand francs myself, so that just leaves sixty-nine and a half million more for you to spend, it's not reaching for the stars with the fortune you've got, but I do need Sir's signature." I exploded: "You've gone completely insane! How can I withdraw seven billion from Worms, even if I take part of it out of my Lazard account?" My manservant was ready with his reply: "I already sorted it out with Renaud de La Martinière, it won't, I promise you, be the least trouble." "The tax authorities are going to be right on it, the police will come after you, there's absolutely no way I'm giving you that money." "Sir is wrong," my manservant replied, "because it's a very good Picasso, truly, Sir would agree, and moreover, it's an excellent investment." "But why do you need a Picasso? You've already got a Greuze, a Hubert Robert, and a Toulouse-Lautrec in your bedroom, isn't that enough for you?" "No, sir, there isn't a Toulouse-Lautrec or a Greuze or a Hubert Robert in my room anymore, because I sold them." "What do you mean? You stole the Greuze, the Hubert Robert, and the Toulouse-Lautrec belonging to my great-grandmother?" "I didn't do it for the money, sir, I had far nobler motives. You hurt my feelings, I was young then, and touchy, I was determined to return the favor. I wasn't stupid, though, if I'd wanted to get the most money I could out of it, you wouldn't believe that I'd gone to the Vanves flea market to sell them off one Saturday morning by passing them off as copies of Lautrec, Hubert Robert, and Greuze." I gasped. "What *did* you do?" "Exactly that, Sir, I always tell Sir the truth." In a blind rage, I leaped to his bedroom door and tried to open it, but he kept me from doing so. We fought. I fell backwards. He dredged me up. The Picasso is splendid. My manservant does have very good taste as well.

I discovered the pleasures of incontinence. At first, it was the last few drops that I wasn't able to hold in anymore when my manservant squatted to pull up my belt. I managed to hide that from him for months. Then I let out little unruly spurts in the warm bathwater, which ended up making me want to pee, so I wouldn't have to get out, hear my shins cracking, and asking for help to reach the icy sink. When he realized what was happening, my manservant said: "If Sir starts peeing in his bath again, I'm not going to let the water drain and Sir can bathe in his cold pee, he can see just how enjoyable that is." He didn't follow through. Ultimately, it was at night, on my couch, because I was all alone, I had a nightmare, I didn't dare wake up my manservant, and suddenly I felt overwhelmingly terrified of the darkness all around. I had been dreaming that a boy wanted to break into my place and that he was saying, behind the door, "It's me, it's Sérafin." I've never known any Sérafin. It flowed down my pajamas, first a warm droplet, it felt like I was crying down there. Now I have bulky, padded underwear that absorbs everything. It's nice and comfortable, I can just unclench my stomach when I want rather than suffer these absurd cramps. My manservant cleans up, I can ask that much of him. "From now on, I won't be calling Sir Sir but Baby, or Sir Baby, because that's what you really are, how does that sound?" Soon it'll be my diarrhea, hotter than the urine.

It's getting harder and harder to write with my lobster-claws. I don't know if I can go on with this story. Might I have to talk into a tape recorder? Or dictate the rest of the book to my manservant? But what will he think of what I think of him? I wouldn't dare to be so honest. There are things I won't have the courage to tell him, I'd be afraid of getting punished. Now I'm convinced that he still hasn't found the notebook, it was just a figment of my imagination, "cynical dandy" is a stock phrase. It's hard for me to imagine these dictation stints that would relieve my hands. I know that my manservant makes very few spelling mistakes when he writes, I've seen it for myself, and that he's capable of nuance, but I don't wholly trust him. Dictating the rest of the bathroom. I didn't want to wake up my manservant. I called for help. He left me on the ground all night. He had his reasons, he said: "You need to know how to be on the ground and not panic, because we don't always have someone around to help get you up. It's a good exercise. I'm not refusing Sir my assistance out of spite, I'll give it, that much he can rest assured of, a bit later, let's say when it's day again, but in the meanwhile, Sir needs to try to calm down and not wriggle around like a crab flipped on its back, there's no point to it." I was furious, I threatened him, I talked down to him imperiously once again: "If you don't call the firefighters or the paramedics, then you're fired." My manservant replied calmly: "I won't be fired because Sir can't do without me anymore. He might have been able to two or three years ago, but now it's too late, we're stuck together to the bitter end. And if I inflict this upon you, believe me, it's not for my pleasure, it's actually very painful for me, it's because I specifically don't want Sir to get into states like this one at a given moment. Sir needs to be serene in order to pass over to the other side, otherwise it'll be hell for you and me both. I'll be as gentle with you as you've always wanted, but for crying out loud, you need to calm down! Dogs sleep just fine on the ground, and so do the Japanese." It's the Japanese all over again. I yelled: "Pull me up right now, or call the firefighters. I might have a cracked rib, a broken spine, I seriously hurt myself when I fell, have you no decency?" "I'm absolutely not calling the firefighters," my manservant retorted, "they're brutes, I'm quite sure you haven't actually broken anything, but the firefighters did come up to our place, they'd certainly find a way to break one of your ribs or spinal discs, they're the worst doctors ever.

Honestly I ought to hate writing. I'd like to be in my manservant's head, to think his thoughts. I'd write better. He's wily, unpredictable, but he's got a heart of gold. When he pricks me, I don't feel this rush of heat anymore bubbling up to my head and coming back down while warming me up all the way to the tips of my toes, I who'd always felt cold there and in my heart and my balls as well. My manservant injects me and it hurts because there's no flesh to prick anymore, but that's all. No pleasure, no relief, no forgetting. I must have developed such a tolerance that it no longer works. Maybe the dose needs to be increased? I'll talk to my doctor about it since he's the one who orders it for me. I feel like my manservant would have pushed him out already if he weren't my supplier, because he knows how much I need this drug. My toes have lost their feeling, apart from cramps or pins and needles, apart from cold. They're not alive anymore. There's no reason for them to be in my Nikes and carrying me around anymore, they're already dead.

I've finally managed to solve the mystery of my manservant's bedroom, because I realized all of a sudden that there had to be a copy of the key on the huge key ring hidden at the bottom of the Ming vase. My manservant always makes sure to lock his bedroom door when he leaves to run errands, and all peering through the keyhole does is mess up my backbone, since he plugged it from the inside with something black. I could have imagined the most madcap or desolate or repugnant things, but not what I actually did see. My great-grandmother's canopy bed had been hacked up with an axe to make the triangular frame of a teepee right in the middle of the empty room, with this axe I'd never seen before lodged at its apex, alongside a huge blood-red feather. There was indeed no trace of the Greuze, or the Toulouse-Lautrec, or the Hubert Robert. Posters of cosmonauts had taken their place. My manservant had rolled up and heaped the rugs in the middle of the teepee to make himself a comfortable bed. I found ashtrays full of cigarette butts and yellowed copies of *Libération*, for the most part issues where the film he'd done was mentioned. Nothing apart from this Sioux tent he slept in. My furniture and tchotchkes were gone, I didn't dare to ask by what witchcraft they'd been vanished. My insistence notwithstanding, as he'd picked it out, he'd refused to keep the Picasso there. He'd hung it in the lounge, above my couch. Had he been hoping that it would fall down and crush my head while I was sleeping?

Henry Mayr-Harting, *Perceptions of Angels in History: An Inaugural Lecture* (Oxford: Clarendon Press, 1998).

Rainer Maria Rilke, *Duino Elegies*, in *The Selected Poetry of Rainer Maria Rilke*, trans. Stephen Mitchell (New York: Vintage, 1989).

Teresa of Avila, *The Life of St Teresa of Jesus, of the Order of Our Lady of Carmel. Written by Herself*, trans. David Lewis (London: Thomas Baker; New York: Benziger Bros, 1904), www.gutenberg.org/ebooks/8120

Tertullian, *Apology*, in Allan Menzies (ed.), *Ante-Nicene Fathers*, vol. iii. *Latin Christianity: Its Founder, Tertullian* (Edinburgh: T&T Clark; Grand Rapids, MI: Eerdmans Publishing Company, 1885), www.ccel.org/ccel/schaff/anf03.html

Chapter 3. What is an angel?

Aristotle, *Aristotle's Metaphysics*, trans. W. D. Ross (2 vols.; Oxford: Clarendon Press, 1924; rev. 1958), http://classics.mit.edu/Aristotle/metaphysics.html

Plato, 'Phaedo', in *Euthyphro, Apology, Crito, and Phaedo*, trans. Benjamin Jowett (Amherst, NY: Prometheus Books, 1988), http://classics.mit.edu/Plato/phaedo.html

Moses Maimonides, *The Guide for the Perplexed*, trans. Michael Friedländer (New York: Hebrew Publishing Company, 1881), http://books.google.co.uk/books?id=e4GgHMPDok0C

Philip Schaff (ed.), *St. Augustin's: City of God and Christian Doctrine* (Nicene and Post-Nicene Fathers First Series Volume 2; Edinburgh: T&T Clark; Michigan: Eerdmans Publishing Company, 1887), www.ccel.org/ccel/schaff/npnf102.html

Thomas Aquinas, *Summa Theologica*, trans. Fathers of the English Dominican (New York: Benziger Bros, 1947), www.newadvent.org/summa

Chapter 4. Divine messengers

Emma Heathcote-James, *Seeing Angels* (London: John Blake Publishing, 2002).

Philip Schaff (ed.), *St Augustin's: City of God and Christian Doctrine* (Nicene and Post-Nicene Fathers First Series Volume 2; Edinburgh: T&T Clark; Michigan: Eerdmans Publishing Company, 1887), www.ccel.org/ccel/schaff/npnf102.html

Chapter 5. Ministering spirits

The Arabian Nights: Tales from a Thousand and One Nights, trans. Richard Burton (New York: Random House Inc., 2001).

David Albert Jones, *The Soul of the Embryo: An Enquiry into the Status of the Human Embryo in the Christian Tradition* (London: Continuum, 2004).

Simon Tugwell, *Human Immortality and the Redemption of Death* (London: Darton, Longman and Todd, 1990).

John Henry Newman, *The Dream of Gerontius* (Oxford: Family Publications, 2001), www.newmanreader.org/works/verses/gerontius.html

Sulpitius Severus, *On The Life of St Martin*, trans. Alexander Roberts, in Philip Schaff and Henry Wace (eds.), *Sulpitius Severus, Vincent of Lerins, John Cassian* (Nicene and Post-Nicene Fathers Second Series Volume 11; Edinburgh: T&T Clark; Michigan: Eerdmans Publishing Company, 1894), www.ccel.org/ccel/schaff/npnf211.html

Salley Vickers, *Miss Garnet's Angel* (London and New York: Harper Perennial, 2006).

Chapter 6. Heavenly hosts

Bryan Appleyard, *Aliens: Why They Are Here* (London: Scribner, 2005).

Thomas Carlyle, *Sartor Resartus* (World Classics; Oxford: Oxford University Press, 1999).

Dionysius, *Celestial Hierarchy*, in *Esoterica*, vol. ii. *148–202* (2000), www.esoteric.msu.edu/VolumeII/CelestialHierarchy.html

Isaac D'Israeli, *Curiosities of Literature: Consisting of Anecdotes, Characters, Sketches, and Observations, Literary, Critical, and Historical* (Printed for J. Murray, 1791; original from Oxford University), www.books.google.co.uk/books?id=rVkUAAAAQAAJ

John Dryden, *The Hind and the Panther*, in Paul Hammond and David Hopkins (eds.), *Dryden: Selected Poems* (Annotated English Poets; London: Longman, 2007).

The Book of Enoch, trans. R. H. Charles (London: SPCK, 1917), www.sacred-texts.com/bib/boe/index.htm

Walter Hilton, *The Scale of Perfection*, trans. John Clark and Rosemary Dorward (Classics of Western Spirituality; New York: Paulist Press, 1990).

Rudolf Otto, *The Idea of the Holy*, trans. John Harvey (New York: Oxford University Press, 1968).

Pascal, *Pensées*, trans. A. Krailsheimer (London: Penguin Classics, 2003).

Philo, *On Dreams, That They Are God-Sent*, in *The Works of Philo: Complete and Unabridged*, New Updated Edition, trans. Charles Duke Yonge (Peabody, MA: Hendrickson Publishers, 1993), www.earlychristianwritings.com/yonge/book21.html (this is a convenient place to find Philo's works, but it should be noted that Philo was a Jew and not an 'early Christian writer')

Rupert Sheldrake and Matthew Fox, *The Physics of Angels: Exploring the Realm Where Science and Spirit Meet* (San Francisco: Harper San Francisco, 1996).

Thomas Aquinas, *Summa Theologica*, trans. Fathers of the English Dominican (New York: Benziger Bros., 1947), www.newadvent.org/summa

Eric von Däniken, *Chariots of the Gods: Was God An Astronaut?* (London: Souvenir Press Ltd, 1990).

Chapter 7. Fallen angels

Clive Staples Lewis, *The Screwtape Letters: Letters from a Senior to a Junior Devil* (Fount edn.; London: HarperCollins, 1998).

Joris-Karl Huysmans, *The Damned (Là-Bas)*, trans. Terry Hale (London: Penguin Classics, 2002).

Philip Schaff (ed.), *St. Augustin's: City of God and Christian Doctrine* (Nicene and Post-Nicene Fathers First Series Volume 2; Edinburgh: T&T Clark; Michigan: Eerdmans Publishing Company, 1887), www.ccel.org/ccel/schaff/npnf102.html

Thomas Aquinas, *Summa Theologica*, trans. Fathers of the English Dominican (New York: Benziger Bros., 1947), www.newadvent.org/summa

Josephus, *Antiquities of the Jews*, in *The Works of Josephus, Complete and Unabridged New Updated Edition*, trans. William Whiston, AM (Peabody, MA: Hendrickson Publishers, 1987), www.ccel.org/ccel/josephus/works/files/works.html

Chapter 8. Wrestling with angels

Doug Beardsley, *Wrestling with Angels: New and Selected Poems 1960–1995* (Montreal and Quebec: Vehicule, 1995).

Phil Blazer and Sherry Portnoy, *Wrestling with the Angels: A History of Jewish Los Angeles* (Encino, CA: Blazer Communications, 2006).

G. K. Chesterton, *Orthodoxy* (San Francisco: Ignatius, 1995).

John J. Clayton, *Wrestling with Angels: New and Collected Stories* (New Milford, CT: Toby Press, 2007).

Marjorie Coppock, *Wrestling with Angels: The Sexual Revolution Confronts the Church* (Eugene, OR: ACW Press, 2003).

Jean-Paul Kauffmann, *The Struggle with the Angel: Delacroix, Jacob, and the God of Good and Evil* (New York: Four Walls Eight Windows, 2002).

Michael King, *Wrestling with the Angel: A Life of Janet Frame* (Auckland: Penguin, 2000).

Elisabeth Kübler-Ross, *On Death and Dying* (New York: Scribner, 1997).

Ehud Luz, *Wrestling with an Angel: Power, Morality, and Jewish Identity*, trans. Michael Swirsky (New Haven: Yale University Press, 2003).

Iris Murdoch, *The Time of the Angels* (London: Vintage, 2002).

Philip Pullman, *The Amber Spyglass* (London: Scholastic, 1995).

Rowan Williams and Mike Higton, *Wrestling with Angels: Conversations in Modern Theology* (London: SCM Press, 2007).

Further reading

Original sources

A good place to start with further reading is with the original sources for stories and speculation about angels. This introduction has included many references to the Jewish Scriptures, the New Testament, and the Quran, so that the reader can follow these up. It is also worth searching the Bible or the Quran, as there are several easily available web-based versions. Two are worth mentioning: the Blue Letter Bible (www.blueletterbible.org) and the Quran Search at IslamiCity (www.islamicity.com/QuranSearch). These are helpful, because they include the original languages and more than one English translation.

There is no searchable version of the Talmud, but there are many references to the Talmud in the excellent article by Ludwig Blau and Kaufman Kohler, 'Angelology', in Cyrus Adler (ed.), *The Jewish Encyclopedia* (New York: Funk and Wagnalls, 1906–10), www.jewishencyclopedia.com/view.jsp?letter=A&artid=1521.

It is then possible to look up the references in a web-based version of the Talmud at www.come-and-hear.com/talmud.

In the References, preference has been given to versions of texts that are available online. However, the newest and most critical editions are not in the public domain. For further reading, see:
James Charlesworth (ed.), *The Old Testament Pseudepigrapha*, vol. i. *Apocalyptic Literature and Testaments* (New Haven: Yale University Press, 1983).

—— *The Old Testament Pseudepigrapha*, vol. ii. *Expansions of the 'Old Testament' and Legends, Wisdom and Philosophical Literature, Prayers, Psalms and Odes, Fragments of lost Judeo-Christian Works* (New Haven: Yale University Press, 1985).

Dionysius, *Pseudo Dionysius: The Complete Works*, trans. Paul Rorem (Classics of Western Spirituality; New York: Paulist Press, 1988).

Thomas Aquinas, *Summa Theologiae*, vol. ix. *Angels: 1a. 50–64*, trans. Kenelm Foster (Cambridge: Cambridge University Press, 2005).

—— *Summa Theologiae*, vol. xv. *The World Order: 1a. 110–119*, trans. M. J. Charlesworth (Cambridge: Cambridge University Press, 2005).

Steven Chase (ed.), *Angelic Spirituality: Medieval Perspectives on the Ways of Angels* (Classics of Western Spirituality) (New York: Paulist Press, 2002).

Angels in art and literature

For academic discussion of angels in art, see:

Charles Dempsey, *Inventing the Renaissance Putto* (Chapel Hill, NC: University of North Carolina Press, 2001).

Glenn Peers, *Subtle Bodies: Representing Angels in Byzantium* (Berkeley, CA, and London: University of California Press, 2001).

Antony Gormley, *Making an Angel* (London: Booth Clibborn, 1998).

Therese Martin, 'The Development of Winged Angels in Early Christian Art', in *Espacio, Tiempo y Forma, Serie VII, Historia del Arte*, 14 (2001), 11–30.

There are also collections of painting of angels with commentary:

Francesco Buranelli and Robin Dietrick, *Between God and Man: Angels in Italian Art* (Jackson, MS: University Press of Mississippi, 2007).

Rosa Geogr, *Angels and Demons in Art*, trans. Rosanna Giammanco Frongia (Oxford: Oxford University Press, 2005).

James Underhill, *Angels* (Shaftesbury and Rockport, MA: Element, 1995).

The collection by Peter Lamborn Wilson, *Angels* (London: Thames and Hudson, 1980) deliberately includes angel-like beings from other traditions.

General surveys of religious art will also include discussion of angels. For example, John Dillenberger, *A Theology of Artistic Sensibilities: The Visual Arts and the Church* (London: SCM Press, 1987).

For more on angels in literature, see:

David Jeffrey, *A Dictionary of Biblical Tradition in English Literature* (Grand Rapids, MI: Wm B. Eerdmans Publishing Company, 1993).

Robert West, 'Angels', in William B Hunter, Jr. (gen. ed.), *A Milton Encyclopedia* (London: Associated University Press, 1978), 48–51.

——*Milton and the Angels* (Athens, GA: University of Georgia Press, 1955).

Angelology

Two very scholarly works on the history of beliefs about angels are:

David Keck, *Angels and Angelology in the Middle Ages* (Oxford: Oxford University Press, 1998).

A. Walsham and P. Marshall, *Angels in the Early Modern World* (Cambridge: Cambridge University Press, 2006).

On the representation of Jesus as an angel, see:

Margaret Barker, The *Great Angel: A Study of Israel's Second God* (Louisville, KY: Westminster John Knox Press, 1992).

Charles Gieschen, *Angelomorphic Christology: Antecedents and Early Evidence* (Leiden, Boston, and Cologne: Brill, 1998).

Peter Carrell, *Jesus and the Angels: Angelology and the Christology of the Apocalypse of John* (Cambridge: Cambridge University Press, 1997).

For those interested in the Christian theology of angels, see:

Karl Rahner, 'Angels', in Karl Rahner (ed.), *Encyclopedia of Theology: The Concise Sacramentum mundi* (London and New York: Continuum International Publishing Group, 1975).

Cornelius Ernst, 'How to See an Angel', in *Multiple Echo: Explorations in Theology* (London: Darton Longman and Todd, 1979).

Peter Williams, *The Case for Angels* (Carlisle: Paternoster, 2002).

There are also a number of more popular Christian works on angels:

Jane Williams, *Angels* (Oxford: Lion Publishing, 2006).

Billy Graham, *Angels: God's Secret Agents* (London: Hodder and Stoughton, 2004).

Martin Israel, *Angels: Messengers of Grace* (London: SPCK, 1995).

Ladislaus Boros, *Angels and Men* (New York: Seabury Press, 1976).

For Muslim and Jewish works on angels, see, for example:

Shaykh Muhammad Hisham Kabbani, *Angels Unveiled: A Sufi Perspective* (Chicago: Kazi Publications, 1996).

Ronald H. Isaacs, *Ascending Jacob's Ladder: Jewish Views of Angels, Demons, and Evil Spirits* (Northvale, NJ: Jason Aronson, 1997).

On Satan, see Jeffrey Burton Russell's five-volume history:

The Devil: Perceptions of Evil from Antiquity to Primitive Christianity (Ithaca, NY: Cornell University Press, 1977).

Satan: The Early Christian Tradition (Ithaca, NY: Cornell University Press, 1981).

Lucifer: The Devil in the Middle Ages (Ithaca, NY: Cornell University Press, 1984).

Mephistopheles: The Devil in the Modern World (Ithaca, NY: Cornell University Press, 1986).

The Prince of Darkness: Radical Evil and the Power of Good in History (Ithaca, NY: Cornell University Press, 1988).

And for those interested in exorcism:

Malachi Martin, *Hostage to the Devil: The Possession and Exorcism of Five Living Americans* (San Francisco: Harper San Francisco, 1992).

Implications

This book grew from an inaugural lecture, David Albert Jones, 'Angels as a Guide to Ethics', *Pastoral Review*, 4/1 (Jan.–Feb. 2008), 11–16.

Mortimer Adler also argues that the idea of angels is helpful in philosophy if we are to avoid angelic fallacies; see *The Angels and Us* (New York: Macmillan Publishing, 1982).

In a slightly different vein, John Cornwell uses the guardian angel as a literary device to offer a gentle critique of Dawkins *Darwin's Angel: An Angelic Riposte to 'The God Delusion'* (London: Profile Books Ltd, 2008).

Index of locorum

Index

Index

Christian Ethics
A Very Short Introduction
D. Stephen Long

This *Very Short Introduction* to Christian ethics introduces the topic by examining its sources and historical basis. D. Stephen Long presents a discussion of the relationship between Christian ethics, modern, and postmodern ethics, and explores practical issues including sex, money, and power. Long recognises the inherent difficulties in bringing together 'Christian' and 'ethics' but argues that this is an important task for both the Christian faith and for ethics. Arguing that Christian ethics are not a precise science, but the cultivation of practical wisdom from a range of sources, Long also discusses some of the failures of the Christian tradition, including the crusades, the conquest, slavery, inquisitions, and the Galileo affair.

www.oup.com/vsi/

mirror, leaning against the sink, he'd watched himself do it. He said: "Oh look, Gramps is in a snit, is he all hot and bothered about his dope getting nicked?" I wanted to slap him, but I couldn't get my arm all the way up to his cheek. He stuck his tongue out at me so I could see what it looked like—swollen, bluish, full of poison—and he ran it harshly along my neck. It was horribly dry and rough, a disgusting velvet.

My manservant claims that tonight, as I slept, I'd screamed, and that I was calling out to Satan, "Sometimes Satan," he said, "sometimes Allah, but never the Good Lord." He was peeved at me the whole day. He says: "I'm no believer, but you don't trespass against Jesus."

I don't get up anymore. I lie there on the ground, huddled up on my side, curled up like a fetus, I'm drooling. My manservant comes to give me my beers and my aquavit, he doesn't hold up my neck anymore as I swallow, I gulp down what I can, it overflows. He doesn't talk to me anymore, and he doesn't answer my questions, apart from kicks that don't hurt too much, I cover my stomach. He says: "Scream all you want, your doctor's never going to warn the police, because he's nose-deep in the white stuff too. You think a morphine addict is going to turn himself in at a police station?" I tremble, I'm in withdrawal, I beg my manservant to give me some again. When he aims another kick at my back or ribs with his combat boots, he says: "Brutality is on the rise everywhere, across the whole world, it's not just here. Don't you read the papers anymore? The other day, in Korea, two fourteen-year-old girls showed up on the side of some road one night, they stopped a car, and forced everyone to get out, there was a grandmother with her five-year-old granddaughter, the two girls made them dig a hole and then buried them alive on the side of the road so they could steal some pocket change. I haven't gone that far with you yet, have I?" He pissed on me, to teach me to be quiet, he said. He'd grown old and ugly, gotten a beer gut. If he had pissed on me when he was fifteen, at a push I might have liked it. But now it's too late, it's just piss that smells like snail juice and goes cold immediately. We don't like each other anymore. That little son of a bitch, that retard, doesn't even hide from me anymore to inject himself, the one in withdrawal now, but shoulders his burden in secret and doesn't let on. The rush from the morphine is all the stronger for my not having taken it for several months, my feet are hot again and there's a velvet buzz around my head. I dictate my book to my manservant, he calmly notes down everything I tell him to write, and doesn't make any comment on it, then I read it myself to make sure he hasn't left anything out. He finally pulled me up and set me down in my ex-bedroom, under the teepee made out of the wood of my great-grandmother's bed. He laid me atop several huge pillows so I could drink without choking. I have to down huge amounts of water. I can't handle beer anymore; I puke it up immediately. I doze and, because of the morphine, I have visions of a sort, at particular moments I'm no longer sure at all whether my manservant is my son or my father. He seems very worried

"Leave me alone. Let me sleep." He protests: "There's no chance I'll let Sir fall into a coma. I'm not upping the doses. I'd rather carry Sir in my arms or on my back through any torment, keep his head above water, until I fall myself. That's why I won't stop talking to Sir, so that your brain keeps on intercepting or interpreting the information I bombard it with. Sir will recall, at Shangri-La, at Bangkok, when we were drinking tequila sunrises and we had those naked ladies, those goddesses dancing right above our heads, spinning around on these phallic metal bars. When they spread their legs, we almost had their bushes right in our noses, did Sir enjoy that?" I mutter, to annoy him: "No, I don't remember that at all. Who are you? I've never seen you around here. Are you part of the firefighting brigade, is that it? Do you save lives? Who let you in?" "It's me, Sir, it's Jim, your manservant." "Kim? Did I find you

Translator's note by

Jeffrey Zuckerman

Translating *My Manservant and Me* was like reuniting with an old friend. The work of selecting and translating many of Hervé Guibert's short stories for *Written in Invisible Ink: Selected Stories* had offered me a long apprenticeship in his style. As I sat down with the final novel published in Guibert's lifetime, I wondered how his illness might have marked his prose. What a relief it was to find his particular turns of phrase, his long yet carefully calibrated sentences, and his barbed sense of humor still intact.

As with Guibert's photographs and his other books, his gestures toward autobiography are practically inseparable from his biting credo that "secrets have to circulate." The narrator of *My Manservant and Me* says he is eighty years old; Guibert himself would have turned eighty in the 2036 mentioned on the final page. But so much of what is unpleasant about the narrator—the incontinence, the casual racism, the immensely controlling instinct that makes him seek out not a genteel valet or a stuffy butler but an outright manservant—seems to be presented for readers to recognize and be repulsed by, exactly like the progression of AIDS in *To the Friend Who Did Not Save My Life*. Even the layout of the text, with large yet consistent gaps between paragraphs, seems deliberately intended to shake readers out of the standard rules of design, along with other forms of complacency.

Indeed, Mathieu Lindon, writing about his friendship with Guibert, remarks that his dear "Hervelino" had "been delighted that I'd read *My Manservant and Me* as a burlesque version of *To the Friend Who Did Not Save My Life*." Death was imminent, and Guibert's body was at the mercy of a disease practically eating him alive. That he could transform the immunodeficiency virus into a manservant who overtakes his master's life is a darkly brilliant joke that makes *My Manservant and Me* an essential text. And translating this work into English, respecting its nuances, its wretchedness, and its sordidness, even as I refashion a deeply French text in my own language, has incarnated the book's best joke of all: the original title, *Mon valet et moi*, is an unmistakable pun on "my manservant *is* me."

—Jeffrey Zuckerman

Hervé Guibert (1955–1991) was a French writer and photographer. A critic for *Le Monde*, he was the author of some thirty books, most notably *To the Friend Who Did Not Save My Life*, which presents an intimate portrait of Michel Foucault and played a significant role in changing public attitudes in France towards AIDS.

Jeffrey Zuckerman is a translator of French, including books by the artists Jean-Michel Basquiat and the Dardenne brothers, the queer writers Jean Genet and Hervé Guibert, and the Mauritian novelists Ananda Devi, Shenaz Patel, and Carl de Souza. A graduate of Yale University, he has been a finalist for the TA First Translation Prize and the French-American Foundation Translation Prize, and has been awarded a PEN/Heim translation grant and the French Voices Grand Prize. In 2020 he was named a Chevalier in the Ordre des Arts et des Lettres by the French government.

NIGHTBOAT BOOKS

Nightboat Books, a nonprofit organization, seeks to develop audiences for writers whose work resists convention and transcends boundaries. We publish books rich with poignancy, intelligence, and risk. Please visit nightboat.org to learn about our titles and how you can support our future publications.

The following individuals have supported the publication of this book. We thank them for their generosity and commitment to the mission of Nightboat Books:

Kazim Ali
Anonymous (4)
Abraham Avnisan
Jean C. Ballantyne
The Robert C. Brooks Revocable Trust
Amanda Greenberger
Rachel Lithgow
Anne Marie Macari
Elizabeth Madans
Elizabeth Motika
Thomas Shardlow
Benjamin Taylor
Jerrie Whitfield & Richard Motika

This book is made possible, in part, by grants from the New York City Department of Cultural Affairs in partnership with the City Council and the New York State Council on the Arts Literature Program.

VERY SHORT INTRODUCTIONS are for anyone wanting a stimulating and accessible way in to a new subject. They are written by experts, and have been published in more than 25 languages worldwide.

The series began in 1995, and now represents a wide variety of topics in history, philosophy, religion, science, and the humanities. The VSI library now contains 300 volumes—a Very Short Introduction to everything from ancient Egypt and Indian philosophy to conceptual art and cosmology—and will continue to grow in a variety of disciplines.

Very Short Introductions available now:

ADVERTISING   Winston Fletcher
AFRICAN HISTORY
   John Parker and Richard Rathbone
AGNOSTICISM   Robin Le Poidevin
AMERICAN IMMIGRATION
   David A. Gerber
AMERICAN POLITICAL PARTIES
   AND ELECTIONS   L. Sandy Maisel
THE AMERICAN PRESIDENCY
   Charles O. Jones
ANARCHISM   Colin Ward
ANCIENT EGYPT   Ian Shaw
ANCIENT GREECE   Paul Cartledge
ANCIENT PHILOSOPHY   Julia Annas
ANCIENT WARFARE
   Harry Sidebottom
ANGELS   David Albert Jones
ANGLICANISM   Mark Chapman
THE ANGLO-SAXON AGE   John Blair
ANIMAL RIGHTS   David DeGrazia
ANTISEMITISM   Steven Beller
THE APOCRYPHAL GOSPELS
   Paul Foster
ARCHAEOLOGY   Paul Bahn
ARCHITECTURE   Andrew Ballantyne
ARISTOCRACY   William Doyle
ARISTOTLE   Jonathan Barnes
ART HISTORY   Dana Arnold
ART THEORY   Cynthia Freeland
ATHEISM   Julian Baggini
AUGUSTINE   Henry Chadwick
AUTISM   Uta Frith

BARTHES   Jonathan Culler
BEAUTY   Roger Scruton
BESTSELLERS   John Sutherland
THE BIBLE   John Riches
BIBLICAL ARCHAEOLOGY
   Eric H. Cline
BIOGRAPHY   Hermione Lee
THE BLUES   Elijah Wald
THE BOOK OF MORMON
   Terryl Givens
THE BRAIN   Michael O'Shea
BRITISH POLITICS   Anthony Wright
BUDDHA   Michael Carrithers
BUDDHISM   Damien Keown
BUDDHIST ETHICS   Damien Keown
CANCER   Nicholas James
CAPITALISM   James Fulcher
CATHOLICISM   Gerald O'Collins
THE CELL   Terence Allen and
   Graham Cowling
THE CELTS   Barry Cunliffe
CHAOS   Leonard Smith
CHOICE THEORY   Michael Allingham
CHRISTIAN ART   Beth Williamson
CHRISTIAN ETHICS   D. Stephen Long
CHRISTIANITY   Linda Woodhead
CITIZENSHIP   Richard Bellamy
CLASSICAL MYTHOLOGY
   Helen Morales
CLASSICS   Mary Beard and
   John Henderson

Available soon:

For more information visit our website
www.oup.com/vsi/